NOW WE ARE
SEVENTY

METHUEN

First published in Great Britain in 1996
by Methuen Children's Books
an imprint of Reed Books Children's Publishing
Michelin House, 81 Fulham Road, London SW3 6RB
and Auckland, Melbourne, Singapore and Toronto.
Copyright © 1996 Michael John Brown, Peter Janson-Smith,
Roger Hugh Vaughan Charles Morgan and
Timothy Michael Robinson, Trustees of the Pooh Properties.
Book design by Mandy Norman
copyright © 1996 Reed International Books Limited.

Now We Are Seventy is a selection of previously
published material taken from:
Winnie-the-Pooh, first published 14 October 1926
text by A.A. Milne and line illustrations by E.H. Shepard
copyright under the Berne Convention.
The House at Pooh Corner, first published 11 October 1928
text by A.A. Milne and line illustrations by E.H. Shepard
copyright under the Berne Convention.
When We Were Very Young, first published 6 November 1924
text by A.A. Milne and line illustrations by E.H. Shepard
copyright under the Berne Convention.
Now We Are Six, first published 13 October 1927
text by A.A. Milne and line illustrations by E.H. Shepard
copyright under the Berne Convention.
"Vespers" , being in the library of the Queen's Dolls' House,
is printed here by special permission.

3 5 7 9 10 8 6 4

ISBN 0 416 19399 4

Printed and bound in Great Britain
by Cox and Wyman Limited, Reading, Berks

CONTENTS

IN WHICH POOH GOES VISITING AND GETS INTO A TIGHT PLACE

1

Edward Bear, known to his friends as Winnie-the-Pooh, or Pooh for short, was walking through the Forest one day, humming proudly to himself. He had made up a little hum that very morning, as he was doing his Stoutness Exercises in front of the glass: *Tra-la-la, tra-la-la*, as he stretched up as high as he could go, and then *Tra-la-la, tra-la-oh, help! -la*, as he tried to reach his toes. After breakfast he had said it over and over to himself until he had learnt it off by heart, and now he was humming it right through, properly. It went like this:

Tra-la-la, tra-la-la,
Tra-la-la, tra-la-la,
Rum-tum-tiddle-um-tum.
Tiddle-iddle, tiddle-iddle,
Tiddle-iddle, tiddle-iddle,
Rum-tum-tum-tiddle-um.

Well, he was humming this hum to himself, and walking gaily along, wondering what everybody else was doing, and what it felt like, being somebody else, when suddenly he came to a sandy bank, and in the bank was a large hole.

"Aha!" said Pooh. (*Rum-tum-tiddle-um-tum.*) "If I

know anything about anything, that hole means Rabbit," he said, "and Rabbit means Company," he said, "and Company means Food and Listening-to-Me-Humming and such like. *Rum-tum-tum-tiddle-um.*"

So he bent down, put his head into the hole, and called out:

"Is anybody at home?"

There was a sudden scuffling noise from inside the hole, and then silence.

"What I said was, 'Is anybody at home?'" called out Pooh very loudly.

"No!" said a voice; and then added, "You needn't shout so loud. I heard you quite well the first time."

"Bother!" said Pooh. "Isn't there anybody here at all?"

"Nobody."

Winnie-the-Pooh took his head out of the hole, and thought for a little, and he thought to himself, "There must be somebody there, because somebody must have *said* 'Nobody.'" So he put his head back in the hole, and said:

"Hallo, Rabbit, isn't that you?"

"No," said Rabbit, in a different sort of voice this time.

"But isn't that Rabbit's voice?"

"I don't *think* so," said Rabbit. "It isn't *meant* to be."

"Oh!" said Pooh.

He took his head out of the hole, and had another think, and then he put it back, and said:

"Well, could you very kindly tell me where Rabbit is?"

"He has gone to see his friend Pooh Bear, who is a great friend of his."

"But this *is* Me!" said Bear, very much surprised.

"What sort of Me?"

"Pooh Bear."

"Are you sure?" said Rabbit, still more surprised.

"Quite, quite sure," said Pooh.

"Oh, well, then, come in."

So Pooh pushed and pushed and pushed his way through the hole, and at last he got in.

"You were quite right," said Rabbit, looking at him all over. "It *is* you. Glad to see you."

"Who did you think it was?"

"Well, I wasn't sure. You know how it is in the Forest. One can't have *anybody* coming into one's house. One has to be *careful*. What about a mouthful of something?"

Pooh always liked a little something at eleven o'clock in the morning, and he was very glad to see Rabbit getting out the plates and mugs; and when Rabbit said, "Honey or condensed milk with your bread?" he was so excited that he said, "Both," and then, so as not to seem greedy, he added, "But don't bother about the bread, please." And for a long time after that he said nothing ... until at last, humming to himself in a rather sticky voice, he got up, shook Rabbit lovingly by the paw, and said that he must be going on.

"Must you?" said Rabbit politely.

"Well," said Pooh, "I could stay a little longer if it – if you –" and he tried very hard to look in the direction of the larder.

"As a matter of fact," said Rabbit, "I was going out myself directly."

"Oh well, then, I'll be going on. Good-bye."

"Well, good-bye, if you're sure you won't have any more."

"*Is* there any more?" asked Pooh quickly.

Rabbit took the covers off the dishes, and said, "No, there wasn't."

"I thought not," said Pooh, nodding to himself. "Well, good-bye. I must be going on."

So he started to climb out of the hole. He pulled with his front paws, and pushed with his back paws, and in a little while his nose was out in the open again ... and then his ears ... and then his front paws ... and then his shoulders ... and then –

"Oh, help!" said Pooh. "I'd better go back."

"Oh, bother!" said Pooh. "I shall have to go on."

"I can't do either!" said Pooh. "Oh, help *and* bother!"

Now, by this time Rabbit wanted to go for a walk too, and finding the front door full, he went out by the back door, and came round to Pooh, and looked at him.

"Hallo, are you stuck?" he asked.

"N-no," said Pooh carelessly. "Just resting and thinking and humming to myself."

"Here, give us a paw."

Pooh Bear stretched out a paw, and Rabbit pulled and pulled and pulled. ...

"*Ow!*" cried Pooh. "You're hurting!"

"The fact is," said Rabbit, "you're stuck."

"It all comes," said Pooh crossly, "of not having front doors big enough."

"It all comes," said Rabbit sternly, "of eating too much. I thought at the time," said Rabbit, "only I didn't like to say anything," said Rabbit, "that one of us was eating too much," said Rabbit, "and I knew it wasn't *me*," he said. "Well, well, I shall go and fetch Christopher Robin."

Christopher Robin lived at the other end of the Forest, and when he came back with Rabbit, and saw the front half of Pooh, he said, "Silly old Bear," in such a loving voice that everybody felt quite hopeful again.

"I was just beginning to think," said Bear, sniffing slightly, "that Rabbit might never be able to use his front door again. And I should *hate* that," he said.

"So should I," said Rabbit.

"Use his front door again?" said Christopher Robin. "Of course he'll use his front door again."

"Good," said Rabbit.

"If we can't pull you out, Pooh, we might push you back."

Rabbit scratched his whiskers thoughtfully, and pointed out that, when once Pooh was pushed back, he was back, and of course nobody was more glad to see Pooh than *he* was, still there it was, some lived in trees and some lived underground, and –

"You mean I'd *never* get out?" said Pooh.

"I mean," said Rabbit, "that having got *so* far, it seems a pity to waste it."

Christopher Robin nodded.

"Then there's only one thing to be done," he said. "We shall have to wait for you to get thin again."

"How long does getting thin take?" asked Pooh anxiously.

"About a week, I should think."

"But I can't stay here for a *week*!"

"You can *stay* here all right, silly old Bear. It's getting you out which is so difficult."

"We'll read to you," said Rabbit cheerfully.

"And I hope it won't snow," he added. "And I say, old fellow, you're taking up a good deal of room in my house – *do* you mind if I use your back legs as a towel-horse? Because, I mean, there they are – doing nothing – and it would be very convenient just to hang the towels on them."

"A week!" said Pooh gloomily. "*What about meals?*"

"I'm afraid no meals," said Christopher Robin, "because of getting thin quicker. But we *will* read to you."

Bear began to sigh, and then found he couldn't because he was so tightly stuck; and a tear rolled down his eye, as he said:

"Then would you read a Sustaining Book, such as would help and comfort a Wedged Bear in Great Tightness?"

So for a week Christopher Robin read that sort of book at the North end of Pooh, and Rabbit hung his washing on the South end ... and in between Bear felt himself getting slenderer and slenderer. And at the end of the week Christopher Robin said, "*Now!*"

So he took hold of Pooh's front paws and Rabbit took hold of Christopher Robin, and all Rabbit's friends and relations took hold of Rabbit, and they all pulled together. ...

And for a long time Pooh only said "*Ow!*" ...

And "*Oh!*" ...

And then, all of a sudden, he said "*Pop!*" just as if a cork were coming out of a bottle.

And Christopher Robin and Rabbit and all Rabbit's friends and relations went head-over-heels backwards ... and on the top of them came Winnie-the-Pooh – free!

So, with a nod of thanks to his friends, he went on with his walk through the forest, humming proudly to himself. But Christopher Robin looked after him lovingly, and said to himself, "Silly old Bear!"

Winnie-The-Pooh

BUCKINGHAM PALACE

They're changing guard at Buckingham Palace –
Christopher Robin went down with Alice.
Alice is marrying one of the guard.
"A soldier's life is terrible hard,"
  Says Alice.

They're changing guard at Buckingham Palace –
Christopher Robin went down with Alice.
We saw a guard in a sentry-box.
"One of the sergeants looks after their socks,"
  Says Alice.

They're changing guard at Buckingham Palace –
Christopher Robin went down with Alice.
We looked for the King, but he never came.
"Well, God take care of him, all the same,"
      Says Alice.

They're changing guard at Buckingham Palace –
Christopher Robin went down with Alice.
They've great big parties inside the grounds.
"I wouldn't be King for a hundred pounds,"
      Says Alice.

They're changing guard at Buckingham Palace –
Christopher Robin went down with Alice.
A face looked out, but it wasn't the King's.
"He's much too busy a-signing things,"
      Says Alice.

They're changing guard at Buckingham Palace –
Christopher Robin went down with Alice.
"Do you think the King knows all about *me*?"
"Sure to, dear, but it's time for tea,"
      Says Alice.

When We Were Very Young

FURRY BEAR

If I were a bear,
    And a big bear too,
I shouldn't much care
    If it froze or snew;
I shouldn't much mind
    If it snowed or friz –
I'd be all fur-lined
    With a coat like his!

For I'd have fur boots and a brown fur wrap,
And brown fur knickers and a big fur cap.
            I'd have a fur muffle-ruff to cover
                my jaws,
                And brown fur mittens on my
                big brown paws.
                With a big brown furry-down
                up to my head,
                I'd sleep all the winter in a big
                fur bed.

14

IN WHICH EEYORE
HAS A BIRTHDAY AND
GETS TWO PRESENTS

2

Eeyore, the old grey Donkey, stood by the side of the stream, and looked at himself in the water.

"Pathetic," he said. "That's what it is. Pathetic."

He turned and walked slowly down the stream for twenty yards, splashed across it, and walked slowly back on the other side. Then he looked at himself in the water again.

"As I thought," he said. "No better from *this* side. But nobody minds. Nobody cares. Pathetic, that's what it is."

There was a crackling noise in the bracken behind him, and out came Pooh.

"Good morning, Eeyore," said Pooh.

"Good morning, Pooh Bear," said Eeyore gloomily. "If it *is* a good morning," he said. "Which I doubt," said he.

"Why, what's the matter?"

"Nothing, Pooh Bear, nothing. We can't all, and some of us don't. That's all there is to it."

"Can't all *what*?" said Pooh, rubbing his nose.

"Gaiety. Song-and-dance. Here we go round the mulberry bush."

"Oh!" said Pooh. He thought for a long time, and then asked, "What mulberry bush is that?"

"Bon-hommy," went on Eeyore gloomily. "French word meaning bonhommy," he explained. "I'm not complaining, but There It Is."

Pooh sat down on a large stone, and tried to think this out. It sounded to him like a riddle, and he was never much good at riddles, being a Bear of Very Little Brain. So he sang *Cottleston Pie* instead:

> *Cottleston, Cottleston, Cottleston Pie,*
> *A fly can't bird, but a bird can fly.*
> *Ask me a riddle and I reply:*
> *"Cottleston, Cottleston, Cottleston Pie."*

That was the first verse. When he had finished it, Eeyore didn't actually say that he didn't like it, so Pooh very kindly sang the second verse to him:

> *Cottleston, Cottleston, Cottleston Pie,*
> *A fish can't whistle and neither can I.*
> *Ask me a riddle and I reply:*
> *"Cottleston, Cottleston, Cottleston Pie."*

Eeyore still said nothing at all, so Pooh hummed the third verse quietly to himself:

> *Cottleston, Cottleston, Cottleston Pie,*
> *Why does a chicken, I don't know why.*
> *Ask me a riddle and I reply:*
> *"Cottleston, Cottleston, Cottleston Pie."*

"That's right," said Eeyore. "Sing. Umty-tiddly, umty-too. Here we go gathering Nuts and May. Enjoy yourself."

"I am," said Pooh.

16   "Some can," said Eeyore.

"Why, what's the matter?"

"*Is* anything the matter?"

"You seem so sad, Eeyore."

"Sad? Why should I be sad? It's my birthday. The happiest day of the year."

"Your birthday?" said Pooh in great surprise.

"Of course it is. Can't you see? Look at all the presents I have had." He waved a foot from side to side. "Look at the birthday cake. Candles and pink sugar."

Pooh looked – first to the right and then to the left.

"Presents?" said Pooh. "Birthday cake?" said Pooh. "*Where?*"

"Can't you see them?"

"No," said Pooh.

"Neither can I," said Eeyore. "Joke," he explained.

"Ha ha!"

Pooh scratched his head, being a little puzzled by all this.

"But is it really your birthday?" he asked.

"It is."

"Oh! Well, many happy returns of the day, Eeyore."

"And many happy returns to you, Pooh Bear."

"But it isn't *my* birthday."

"No, it's mine."

"But you said 'Many happy returns' –"

"Well, why not? You don't always want to be miserable on my birthday, do you?"

"Oh I see," said Pooh.

17

"It's bad enough," said Eeyore, almost breaking down, "being miserable myself, what with no presents and no cake and no candles, and no proper notice taken of me at all, but if everybody else is going to be miserable too –"

This was too much for Pooh. "Stay there!" he called to Eeyore, as he turned and hurried back home as quick as he could; for he felt that he must get poor Eeyore a present of *some* sort at once, and he could always think of a proper one afterwards.

Outside his house he found Piglet, jumping up and down trying to reach the knocker.

"Hallo, Piglet," he said.

"Hallo, Pooh," said Piglet.

"What are *you* trying to do?"

"I was trying to reach the knocker," said Piglet. "I just came round –"

"Let me do it for you," said Pooh kindly. So he reached up and knocked at the door. "I have just seen Eeyore," he began, "and poor Eeyore is in a Very Sad Condition, because it's his birthday, and nobody has taken any notice of it, and he's very Gloomy – you know what Eeyore is – and there he was, and – What a long time whoever lives here is answering this door.

And he knocked again.

"But Pooh," said Piglet, "it's your own house!"

"Oh!" said Pooh. "So it is," he said. "Well, let's go in."

So in they went. The first thing Pooh did was to go to the cupboard to see if he had quite a small jar of honey left; and he had, so he took it down.

"I'm giving this to Eeyore," he explained, "as a present. What are *you* going to give?"

"Couldn't I give it too?" said Piglet. "From both of us?"

"No," said Pooh. "That would *not* be a good plan."

"All right, then, I'll give him a balloon. I've got one left from my party. I'll go and get it now, shall I?"

"That, Piglet, is a *very* good idea. It is just what Eeyore wants to cheer him up. Nobody can be uncheered with a balloon."

So off Piglet trotted; and in the other direction went Pooh, with his jar of honey.

It was a warm day, and he had a long way to go. He hadn't gone more than half-way when a sort of funny feeling began to creep all over him. It began at the tip of his nose and trickled all through him and out at the soles of his feet. It was just as if somebody inside him were saying, "Now then, Pooh, time for a little something."

"Dear, dear," said Pooh, "I didn't know it was as late as that." So he sat down and took the top off his jar of honey. "Lucky I brought this with me," he thought. "Many a bear going out on a warm day like this would never have thought of bringing a little something with him." 19

And he began to eat.

"Now let me see," he thought, as he took his last lick of the inside of the jar, "where was I going? Ah, yes, Eeyore." He got up slowly.

And then, suddenly, he remembered. He had eaten Eeyore's birthday present! "*Bother!*" said Pooh. "What *shall* I do? I *must* give him *something*."

For a little while he couldn't think of anything. Then he thought: "Well, it's a very nice pot, even if there's no honey in it, and if I washed it clean, and got somebody to write '*A Happy Birthday*' on it, Eeyore could keep things in it, which might be Useful." So, as he was just passing the Hundred Acre Wood, he went inside to call on Owl, who lived there.

"Good morning, Owl," he said.

"Good morning, Pooh," said Owl.

"Many happy returns of Eeyore's birthday," said Pooh.

"Oh, is that what it is?"

"What are you giving him, Owl?"

"What are *you* giving him, Pooh?"

"I'm giving him a Useful Pot to Keep Things In, and I wanted to ask you –"

"Is this it?" said Owl, taking it out of Pooh's paw.

"Yes, and I wanted to ask you –"

"Somebody has been keeping honey in it," said Owl.

"You can keep *anything* in it," said Pooh earnestly. "It's Very Useful like that. And I wanted to ask you –"

"You ought to write '*A Happy Birthday*' on it."

"*That* was what I wanted to ask you," said Pooh. "Because my spelling is Wobbly. It's good spelling but it

Wobbles, and the letters get in the wrong places. Would *you* write 'A Happy Birthday' on it for me?"

"It's a nice pot," said Owl, looking at it all round. "Couldn't I give it too? From both of us?"

"No," said Pooh. "That would *not* be a good plan. Now I'll just wash it first, and then you can write on it."

Well, he washed the pot out, and dried it, while Owl licked the end of his pencil, and wondered how to spell 'birthday'.

"Can you read, Pooh?" he asked a little anxiously. "There's a notice about knocking and ringing outside my door, which Christopher Robin wrote. Could you read it?"

"Christopher Robin told me what it said, and *then* I could."

"Well, I'll tell you what *this* says, and then you'll be able to."

So Owl wrote ... and this is what he wrote:

HIPY PAPY BTHUTHDTH THUTHDA
BTHUTHDY.

Pooh looked on admiringly.

"I'm just saying 'A Happy Birthday'," said Owl carelessly.

"It's a nice long one," said Pooh, very much impressed by it.

"Well, *actually*, of course, I'm saying 'A very Happy Birthday with love from Pooh.' Naturally it takes a good deal of pencil to say a long thing like that."

"Oh, I see," said Pooh.

While all this was happening, Piglet had gone back to his own house to get Eeyore's balloon. He held it very tightly against himself, so that it shouldn't blow away, and he ran as fast as he could so as to get to Eeyore before Pooh did; for he thought that he would like to be the first one to give a present, just as if he had thought of it without being told by anybody. And running along, and thinking how pleased Eeyore would be, he didn't look where he was going ... and suddenly he put his foot in a rabbit hole, and fell down flat on his face.

BANG!!!???***!!!

 Piglet lay there, wondering what had happened. At first he thought that the whole world had blown up; and then he thought that perhaps only the Forest part of it had; and then he thought that perhaps only *he* had, and he was now alone in the moon or somewhere, and would never see Christopher Robin or Pooh or Eeyore again. And then he thought, "Well, even if I'm in the moon, I needn't be face downwards all the time," so he got cautiously up and looked about him.

He was still in the Forest!

"Well, that's funny," he thought. "I wonder what that bang was. I couldn't have made such a noise just falling down. And where's my balloon? And what's that small piece of damp rag doing?"

It was the balloon!

"Oh, dear!" said Piglet. "Oh, dear, oh, dearie, dearie, dear! Well, it's too late now. I can't go back, and I haven't another balloon, and perhaps Eeyore doesn't *like* balloons so *very* much."

So he trotted on, rather sadly now, and down he came to the side of the stream where Eeyore was, and called out to him.

"Good morning, Eeyore," shouted Piglet.

"Good morning, Little Piglet," said Eeyore. "If it *is* a good morning," he said. "Which I doubt," said he. "Not that it matters," he said.

"Many happy returns of the day," said Piglet, having now got closer.

Eeyore stopped looking at himself in the stream, and turned to stare at Piglet.

"Just say that again," he said.

"Many hap –"

"Wait a moment."

Balancing on three legs, he began to bring his fourth leg very cautiously up to his ear. "I did this yesterday," he explained, as he fell down for the third time. "It's quite easy. It's so as I can hear better. ... There, that's done it! Now then, what were you saying?" He pushed his ear forward with his hoof.

"Many happy returns of the day," said Piglet again.

"Meaning me?"

"Of course, Eeyore."

"My birthday?"

"Yes."

"Me having a real birthday?"

"Yes, Eeyore, and I've brought you a present."

Eeyore took down his right hoof from his right ear, turned round, and with great difficulty put up his left hoof.

"I must have that in the other ear," he said. "Now then."

"A present," said Piglet very loudly.

"Meaning me again?"

"Yes."

"My birthday still?"

"Of course, Eeyore."

"Me going on having a real birthday?"

"Yes, Eeyore, and I brought you a balloon."

"*Balloon*?" said Eeyore. "You did say balloon? One of those big coloured things you blow up? Gaiety, song-and-dance, here we are and there we are?"

"Yes, but I'm afraid – I'm very sorry, Eeyore – but when I was running along to bring it you, I fell down."

"Dear, dear, how unlucky! You ran too fast, I expect. You didn't hurt yourself, Little Piglet?"

"No, but I – I – oh, Eeyore, I burst the balloon!"

There was a very long silence.

"My balloon?" said Eeyore at last.

Piglet nodded.

"My birthday balloon?"

"Yes, Eeyore," said Piglet, sniffing a little. "Here it is. With – with many happy returns of the day." And he gave Eeyore the small piece of damp rag.

"Is this it?" said Eeyore, a little surprised.

Piglet nodded.

"My present?"

Piglet nodded again.

"The balloon?"

"Yes."

"Thank you, Piglet," said Eeyore. "You don't mind my asking," he went on, "but what colour was this balloon when it – when it *was* a balloon?"

"Red."

"I just wondered. ... Red," he murmured to himself. "My favourite colour. ... How big was it?"

"About as big as me."

"I just wondered. ... About as big as Piglet," he said to himself sadly. "My favourite size. Well, well."

Piglet felt very miserable, and didn't know what to say. He was still opening his mouth to begin something, and then deciding that it wasn't any good saying *that*, when he heard a shout from the other side of the river, and there was Pooh.

"Many happy returns of the day," called out Pooh, forgetting that he had said it already.

"Thank you, Pooh, I'm having them," said Eeyore gloomily.

"I've brought you a little present," said Pooh excitedly.

"I've had it," said Eeyore.

Pooh had now splashed across the stream to Eeyore, and Piglet was sitting a little way off, his head in his paws, snuffling to himself.

"It's a Useful Pot," said Pooh. "Here it is. And it's got 'A Very Happy Birthday with love from Pooh' written on it. 25

That's what all that writing is. And it's for putting things in. There!"

When Eeyore saw the pot, he became quite excited.

"Why!" he said. "I believe my balloon will just go into that Pot!"

"Oh, no, Eeyore," said Pooh. "Balloons are much too big to go into Pots. What you do with a balloon is, you hold the balloon –"

"Not mine," said Eeyore proudly. "Look, Piglet!" And as Piglet looked sorrowfully round, Eeyore picked the balloon up with his teeth, and placed it carefully in the pot; picked it out and put it on the ground; and then picked it up again and put it carefully back.

"So it does!" said Pooh. "It goes in!"

"So it does!" said Piglet. "And it comes out!"

"Doesn't it?" said Eeyore. "It goes in and out like anything."

"I'm very glad," said Pooh happily, "that I thought of giving you a Useful Pot to put things in."

"I'm very glad," said Piglet happily, "that I thought of giving you Something to put in a Useful Pot."

But Eeyore wasn't listening. He was taking the balloon out, and putting it back again, as happy as could be. . . .

"And didn't *I* give him anything?" asked Christopher Robin sadly.

"Of course you did," I said. "You gave him – don't you remember – a little – a little –"

"I gave him a box of paints to paint things with."

"That was it."

"Why didn't I give it to him in the morning?"

"You were so busy getting his party ready for him. He had a cake with icing on the top, and three candles, and his name in pink sugar, and –"

"Yes, *I* remember," said Christopher Robin.

Winnie-The-Pooh

HALFWAY DOWN

Halfway down the stairs
Is a stair
Where I sit.
There isn't any
Other stair
Quite like
It.

I'm not at the bottom,
I'm not at the top;
So this is the stair
Where
I always
Stop.

Halfway up the stairs
Isn't up,
And isn't down.
It isn't in the nursery,
It isn't in the town.
And all sorts of funny thoughts
Run round my head:
"It isn't really
Anywhere!
It's somewhere else
Instead!"

VESPERS

Little Boy kneels at the foot of the bed,
Droops on the little hands little gold head.
Hush! Hush! Whisper who dares!
Christopher Robin is saying his prayers.

God bless Mummy. I know that's right.
Wasn't it fun in the bath to-night?
The cold's so cold, and the hot's so hot.
Oh! God bless Daddy – I quite forgot.

If I open my fingers a little bit more,
I can see Nanny's dressing-gown on the door.
It's a beautiful blue, but it hasn't a hood.
Oh! *God bless Nanny and make her good.*

Mine has a hood, and I lie in bed,
And pull the hood right over my head,
And I shut my eyes, and I curl up small,
And nobody knows that I'm there at all.

Oh! *Thank you, God, for a lovely day.*
And what was the other I had to say?
I said "Bless Daddy," so what can it be?
Oh! Now I remember it. *God bless Me.*

Little Boy kneels at the foot of the bed,
Droops on the little hands little gold head.
Hush! Hush! Whisper who dares!
Christopher Robin is saying his prayers.

THE FRIEND

There are lots and lots of people who are always
    asking things,
Like Dates and Pounds-and-ounces and the names
    of funny Kings,
And the answer's either Sixpence or A Hundred
    Inches Long.
And I know they'll think me silly if I get the answer
    wrong.

So Pooh and I go whispering, and Pooh looks very
    bright,
And says, "Well, *I* say sixpence, but I don't suppose
    I'm right."
And then it doesn't matter what the answer ought
    to be,
'Cos if he's right, I'm Right, and if he's wrong, it
    isn't Me.

Now We Are Six

IN WHICH TIGGER COMES TO THE FOREST AND HAS BREAKFAST

3

Winnie-the-Pooh woke up suddenly in the middle of the night and listened. Then he got out of bed, and lit his candle and stumped across the room to see if anybody was trying to get into his honey-cupboard, and they weren't, so he stumped back again, blew out his candle, and got into bed. Then he heard the noise again.

"Is that you, Piglet?" he said.

But it wasn't.

"Come in, Christopher Robin," he said.

But Christopher Robin didn't.

"Tell me about it to-morrow, Eeyore," said Pooh sleepily.

But the noise went on.

"*Worraworraworraworraworra*," said Whatever-it-was, and Pooh found that he wasn't asleep after all.

"What can it be?" he thought. "There are lots of noises in the Forest, but this is a different one. It isn't a growl, and it isn't a purr, and it isn't a bark, and it isn't the noise-you-make-before-beginning-a-piece-of-poetry, but it's a noise of some kind, made by a strange animal! And he's making it outside my door. So I shall get up and ask him not to do it."

He got out of bed and opened his front door.

"Hallo!" said Pooh, in case there was anything outside.

"Hallo!" said Whatever-it-was.

"Oh!" said Pooh. "Hallo!"

"Hallo!"

"Oh, *there* you are!" said Pooh. "Hallo!"

"Hallo!" said the Strange Animal, wondering how long this was going on.

Pooh was just going to say "Hallo!" for the fourth time when he thought that he wouldn't, so he said, "Who is it?" instead.

"Me," said a voice.

"Oh!" said Pooh. "Well, come here."

So Whatever-it-was came here, and in the light of the candle he and Pooh looked at each other.

"I'm Pooh," said Pooh.

"I'm Tigger," said Tigger.

"Oh!" said Pooh, for he had never seen an animal like this before. "Does Christopher Robin know about you?"

"Of course he does," said Tigger.

"Well," said Pooh, "it's the middle of the night, which is a good time for going to sleep. And to-morrow morning we'll have some honey for breakfast. Do Tiggers like honey?"

"They like everything," said Tigger cheerfully.

"Then if they like going to sleep on the floor, I'll go back to bed," said Pooh, "and we'll do things in the morning. Good night." And he got back into bed and went fast asleep.

When he awoke in the morning, the first thing he saw was Tigger, sitting in front of the glass and looking at himself.

"Hallo!" said Pooh.

"Hallo!" said Tigger. "I've found somebody just like me. I thought I was the only one of them."

Pooh got out of bed, and began to explain what a looking-glass was, but just as he was getting to the interesting part, Tigger said:

"Excuse me a moment,

but there's something climbing up your table," and with one loud *Worraworraworraworraworra* he jumped at the end of the tablecloth, pulled it to the ground, wrapped 35 himself up in it three times, rolled to the other end of the room, and, after a terrible struggle, got his head into the daylight again, and said cheerfully: "Have I won?"

"That's my tablecloth," said Pooh, as he began to unwind Tigger.

"I wondered what it was," said Tigger.

"It goes on the table and you put things on it."

"Then why did it try to bite me when I wasn't looking?"

"I don't *think* it did," said Pooh.

"It tried," said Tigger, "but I was too quick for it."

Pooh put the cloth back on the table, and he put a large honey-pot on the cloth, and they sat down to breakfast. And as soon as they sat down, Tigger took a large mouthful of honey ... and he looked up at the ceiling with his head on one side, and made exploring noises with his tongue, and considering noises, and what-have-we-got-*here* noises ... and then he said in a very decided voice:

"Tiggers don't like honey."

"Oh!" said Pooh, and tried to make it sound Sad and Regretful. "I thought they liked everything."

"Everything except honey," said Tigger.

Pooh felt rather pleased about this, and said that, as soon as he had finished his own breakfast, he would take Tigger round to Piglet's house, and Tigger could try some of Piglet's haycorns.

"Thank you, Pooh," said Tigger, "because haycorns is really what Tiggers like best."

So after breakfast they went round to see Piglet, and Pooh explained as they went that Piglet was a Very Small Animal who didn't like bouncing, and asked Tigger not to be too Bouncy just at first. And Tigger, who had been hiding behind trees and jumping out on Pooh's shadow when it wasn't looking, said that Tiggers were only bouncy before breakfast, and that as soon as they had had a few haycorns they became Quiet and Refined. So by-and-by they knocked at the door of Piglet's house.

"Hallo, Pooh," said Piglet.

"Hallo, Piglet. This is Tigger."

"Oh, is it?" said Piglet, and he edged round to the other side of the table. "I thought Tiggers were smaller than that."

"Not the big ones," said Tigger.

"They like haycorns," said Pooh, "so that's what we've come for, because poor Tigger hasn't had any breakfast yet."

Piglet pushed the bowl of haycorns towards Tigger, and said, "Help yourself," and then he got close up to Pooh and felt much braver, and said, "So you're Tigger? Well, well!" in a careless sort of voice. But Tigger said nothing because 37 his mouth was full of haycorns....

After a long munching noise he said:

"Ee-ers o i a-ors."

And when Pooh and Piglet said "What?" he said "Skoos ee," and went outside for a moment.

When he came back he said firmly:

"Tiggers don't like haycorns."

"But you said they liked everything except honey," said Pooh.

"Everything except honey *and* haycorns," explained Tigger.

When he heard this, Pooh said, "Oh, I see!" and Piglet, who was rather glad that Tiggers didn't like haycorns, said, "What about thistles?"

"Thistles," said Tigger, "is what Tiggers like best."

"Then let's go along and see Eeyore," said Piglet.

So the three of them went; and after they had walked and walked and walked, they came to the part of the Forest where Eeyore was.

"Hallo, Eeyore!" said Pooh. "This is Tigger."

"What is?" said Eeyore.

"This," explained Pooh and Piglet together, and Tigger smiled his happiest smile and said nothing.

Eeyore walked all round Tigger one way, and then turned and walked all round him the other way.

"What did you say it was?" he asked.

"Tigger."

"Ah!" said Eeyore.

"He's just come," explained Piglet.

"Ah!" said Eeyore again.

He thought for a long time and then said:

38

"When is he going?"

Pooh explained to Eeyore that Tigger was a great friend of Christopher Robin's, who had come to stay in the Forest, and Piglet explained to Tigger that he mustn't mind what Eeyore said because he was *always* gloomy; and Eeyore explained to Piglet that, on the contrary, he was feeling particularly cheerful this morning; and Tigger explained to anybody who was listening that he hadn't had any breakfast yet.

"I knew there was something," said Pooh. "Tiggers always eat thistles, so that was why we came to see you, Eeyore."

"Don't mention it, Pooh."

"Oh, Eeyore, I didn't mean that I didn't *want* to see you –"

"Quite – quite. But your new stripy friend – naturally, he wants his breakfast. What did you say his name was?"

"Tigger."

"Then come this way, Tigger."

Eeyore led the way to the most thistly-looking patch of thistles that ever was, and waved a hoof at it.

"A little patch I was keeping for my birthday," he said, "but, after all, what *are* birthdays? Here to-day and gone to-morrow. Help yourself, Tigger."

Tigger thanked him and looked a little anxiously at Pooh.

"Are these really thistles?" he whispered.

"Yes," said Pooh.

"What Tiggers like best?"

"That's right," said Pooh.

"I see," said Tigger.

So he took a large mouthful, and he gave a large crunch.

"*Ow!*" said Tigger.

He sat down and put his paw in his mouth.

"What's the matter?" asked Pooh.

"*Hot!*" mumbled Tigger.

"Your friend," said Eeyore, "appears to have bitten on a bee."

Pooh's friend stopped shaking his head to get the prickles out, and explained that Tiggers didn't like thistles.

"Then why bend a perfectly good one?" asked Eeyore.

"But you said," began Pooh, "– you *said* that Tiggers liked everything except honey and haycorns."

"*And* thistles," said Tigger, who was now running round in circles with his tongue hanging out.

Pooh looked at him sadly.

"What are we going to do?" he asked Piglet.

Piglet knew the answer to that, and he said at once that they must go and see Christopher Robin.

"You'll find him with Kanga," said Eeyore. He came close to Pooh, and said in a loud whisper:

"*Could* you ask your friend to do his exercises somewhere else? I shall be having lunch directly, and don't want it bounced on just before I begin. A trifling matter, and fussy of me, but we all have our little ways."

Pooh nodded solemnly and called to Tigger.

"Come along and we'll go and see Kanga. She's sure to have lots of breakfast for you."

Tigger finished his last circle and came up to Pooh and Piglet.

"Hot!" he explained with a large and friendly smile. "Come on!" and he rushed off.

Pooh and Piglet walked slowly after him. And as they walked Piglet said nothing, because he couldn't think of anything, and Pooh said nothing, because he was thinking of a poem. And when he had thought of it he began:

> *What shall we do about poor little Tigger?*
> *If he never eats nothing he'll never get bigger.*
> *He doesn't like honey and haycorns and thistles*
> *Because of the taste and because of the bristles.*
> *And all the good things which an animal likes*
> *Have the wrong sort of swallow or too many spikes.*

"He's quite big enough anyhow," said Piglet.

"He isn't *really* very big."

"Well, he *seems* so."

Pooh was thoughtful when he heard this, and then he murmured to himself:

> *But whatever his weight in pounds, shillings, and ounces,*
> *He always seems bigger because of his bounces.*

42   "And that's the whole poem," he said. "Do you like it, Piglet?"

"All except the shillings," said Piglet. "I don't think they ought to be there."

"They wanted to come in after the pounds," explained Pooh, "so I let them. It is the best way to write poetry, letting things come."

"Oh, I didn't know," said Piglet.

Tigger had been bouncing in front of them all this time, turning round every now and then to ask, "Is this the way?" – and now at last they came in sight of Kanga's house, and there was Christopher Robin. Tigger rushed up to him.

"Oh, there you are, Tigger!" said Christopher Robin. "I knew you'd be somewhere."

"I've been finding things in the Forest," said Tigger importantly. "I've found a pooh and a piglet and an eeyore, but I can't find any breakfast."

Pooh and Piglet came up and hugged Christopher Robin, and explained what had been happening.

"Don't *you* know what Tiggers like?" asked Pooh.

"I expect if I thought very hard I should," said Christopher Robin, "but I *thought* Tigger knew."

"I do," said Tigger. "Everything there is in the world except honey and haycorns and – what were those hot things called?"

"Thistles."

"Yes, and those."

"Oh, well then, Kanga can give you some breakfast."

So they went into Kanga's house, and when Roo had said, "Hallo, Pooh," and "Hallo, Piglet" once, and "Hallo, Tigger" twice, because he had never said it before and it sounded funny, they told Kanga what they wanted, and 43

Kanga said very kindly, "Well, look in my cupboard, Tigger dear, and see what you'd like." Because she knew at once that, however big Tigger seemed to be, he wanted as much kindness as Roo.

"Shall I look, too?" said Pooh, who was beginning to feel

a little eleven o'clockish. And he found a small tin of condensed milk, and something seemed to tell him that Tiggers didn't like this, so he took it into a corner by itself, and went with it to see that nobody interrupted it.

But the more Tigger put his nose into this and his paw into that, the more things he found which Tiggers didn't like. And when he had found everything in the cupboard, and couldn't eat any of it, he said to Kanga, "What happens now?"

But Kanga and Christopher Robin and Piglet were all standing round Roo, watching him have his Extract of Malt. And Roo was saying, "Must I?" and Kanga was saying,

"Now, Roo dear, you remember what you promised."

"What is it?" whispered Tigger to Piglet.

"His Strengthening Medicine," said Piglet. "He hates it."

So Tigger came closer, and he leant over the back of Roo's chair, and suddenly he put out his tongue, and took one large galollop, and, with a sudden jump of surprise, Kanga said, "Oh!" and then clutched at the spoon again just as it was disappearing, and pulled it safely back out of Tigger's mouth. But the Extract of Malt had gone.

"Tigger *dear*!" said Kanga.

"He's taken my medicine, he's taken my medicine, he's taken my medicine!" sang Roo happily, thinking it was a tremendous joke.

Then Tigger looked up at the ceiling, and closed his eyes, and his tongue went round and round his chops, in case he had left any outside, and a peaceful smile came over his face as he said, "So *that's* what Tiggers like!"

* * * *

Which explains why he always lived at Kanga's house afterwards, and had Extract of Malt for breakfast, dinner, and tea. And sometimes, when Kanga thought he wanted strengthening, he had a spoonful or two of Roosbreakfast after meals as medicine.

"But *I* think," said Piglet to Pooh, "that he's been strengthened quite enough."

US TWO

Wherever I am, there's always Pooh,
There's always Pooh and Me.
Whatever I do, he wants to do,
"Where are you going today?" says Pooh:
"Well, that's very odd 'cos I was too.
Let's go together," says Pooh, says he.
"Let's go together," says Pooh.

"What's twice eleven?" I said to Pooh,
("Twice what?" said Pooh to Me.)
"I *think* it ought to be twenty-two."
"Just what I think myself," said Pooh.
"It wasn't an easy sum to do,
But that's what it is," said Pooh, said he.
"That's what it is," said Pooh.

"Let's look for dragons," I said to Pooh.
"Yes, let's," said Pooh to Me.
We crossed the river and found a few –
"Yes, those are dragons all right," said Pooh.
"As soon as I saw their beaks I knew.
That's what they are," said Pooh, said he.
"That's what they are," said Pooh.

"Let's frighten the dragons," I said to Pooh.
"That's right," said Pooh to Me.
"*I'm* not afraid," I said to Pooh,
And I held his paw and I shouted, "Shoo!
Silly old dragons!" – and off they flew.
"I wasn't afraid," said Pooh, said he,
"I'm *never* afraid with you."

So wherever I am, there's always Pooh,
There's always Pooh and Me.
"What would I do?" I said to Pooh,
"If it wasn't for you," and Pooh said: "True,
It isn't much fun for One, but Two
Can stick together," says Pooh, says he.
"That's how it is," says Pooh.

Now We Are Six

IN WHICH CHRISTOPHER ROBIN AND POOH COME TO AN ENCHANTED PLACE AND WE LEAVE THEM THERE

4

Christopher Robin was going away. Nobody knew why he was going; nobody knew where he was going; indeed, nobody even knew why he knew that Christopher Robin *was* going away. But somehow or other everybody in the Forest felt that it was happening at last. Even Smallest-of-all, a friend-and-relation of Rabbit's who thought he had once seen Christopher Robin's foot, but couldn't quite be sure because perhaps it was something else, even S. of A. told himself that Things were going to be Different; and Late and Early, two other friends-and-relations, said, "Well, Early?" and "Well, Late?" to each other in such a hopeless sort of way that it really didn't seem any good waiting for the answer.

One day when he felt that he couldn't wait any longer, Rabbit brained out a Notice, and this is what it said:

"Notice a meeting of everybody will meet at the House at Pooh Corner to pass a Rissolution By Order Keep to the Left Signed Rabbit."

He had to write this out two or three times before he could get the rissolution to look like what he thought it was going to when he began to spell it; but, when at last it was finished, he took it round to everybody and read it out to them. And they all said they would come.

"Well," said Eeyore that afternoon, when he saw them all   49 walking up to his house, "this *is* a surprise. Am *I* asked too?"

"Don't mind Eeyore," whispered Rabbit to Pooh. "I told him all about it this morning."

Everybody said "How-do-you-do" to Eeyore, and Eeyore said that he didn't, not to notice, and then they sat down; and as soon as they were all sitting down, Rabbit stood up again.

"We all know why we're here," he said, "but I have asked my friend Eeyore –"

"That's Me," said Eeyore. "Grand."

"I have asked him to Propose a Rissolution." And he sat down again. "Now then, Eeyore," he said.

"Don't Bustle me," said Eeyore, getting up slowly. "Don't now-then me." He took a piece of paper from behind his ear, and unfolded it. "Nobody knows anything about this," he went on. "This is a Surprise." He coughed in an important way, and

50 began again: "What-nots and

Etceteras, before I begin, or perhaps I should say, before I end, I have a piece of Poetry to read to you. Hitherto – hitherto – a long word meaning – well, you'll see what it means directly – hitherto, as I was saying, all the Poetry in the Forest has been written by Pooh, a Bear with a Pleasing Manner but a Positively Startling Lack of Brain. The Poem which I am now about to read to you was written by Eeyore, or Myself, in a Quiet Moment. If somebody will take Roo's bull's eye away from him, and wake up Owl, we shall all be able to enjoy it. I call it – POEM."

This was it:

> Christopher Robin is going.
> At least I think he is.
> Where?
> Nobody knows.
> But he is going –
> I mean he goes
> (To rhyme with "knows")
> Do we care?
> (To rhyme with "where")
> We do
> Very much.
> (I haven't got a rhyme for that "is"
> in the second line yet. Bother.)
> (Now I haven't got a rhyme for
> bother. Bother).
> Those two bothers will have to
> rhyme with each other
> Buther.
> The fact is this is more difficult
> than I thought,

Pooh

WOL

I ought –
(Very good indeed)
I ought
To begin again,
But it is easier
To stop.
Christopher Robin, good-bye,
I
(Good)
I
And all your friends
Sends –
I mean all your friend
Send –
(Very awkward this, it keeps going wrong.)
Well, anyhow, we send
Our love
END.

"If anybody wants to clap," said Eeyore when he had read this, "now is the time to do it."

They all clapped.

"Thank you," said Eeyore. "Unexpected and gratifying, if a little lacking in Smack."

"It's much better than mine," said Pooh admiringly, and he really thought it was.

"Well," explained Eeyore modestly, "it was meant to be."

"The rissolution," said Rabbit, "is that we all sign it, and take it to Christopher Robin."

So it was signed POOH, WOL, PIGLET, EOR, RABBIT, KANGA, BLOT, SMUDGE, and they all went off to Christopher Robin's house with it.

"Hallo, everybody," said Christopher Robin – "Hallo, Pooh."

They all said "Hallo," and felt awkward and unhappy suddenly, because it was a sort of good-bye they were saying, and they didn't want to think about it. So they stood around, and waited for somebody else to speak, and they nudged each other, and said "Go on," and gradually Eeyore was nudged to the front, and the others crowded behind him.

"What is it, Eeyore?" asked Christopher Robin.

Eeyore swished his tail from side to side, so as to encourage himself, and began.

"Christopher Robin," he said, "we've come to say – to give you – it's called – written by – but we've all – because we've heard, I mean we all know – well, you see, it's – we – you – well, that, to put it as shortly as possible, is what it is." He turned round angrily on the others and said, 53

"Everybody crowds round so in this Forest. There's no Space. I never saw a more Spreading lot of animals in my life, and all in the wrong places. Can't you *see* that Christopher Robin wants to be alone? I'm going." And he humped off.

Not quite knowing why, the others began edging away, and when Christopher Robin had finished reading POEM, and was looking up to say "Thank you," only Pooh was left.

"It's a comforting sort of thing to have," said Christopher Robin, folding up the paper, and putting it in his pocket. "Come on, Pooh," and he walked off quickly.

"Where are we going?" said Pooh, hurrying after him, and wondering whether it was to be an Explore or a What-shall-I-do-about-you-know-what.

"Nowhere," said Christopher Robin.

So they began going there, and after they had walked a little way Christopher Robin said:

"What do you like doing best in the world, Pooh?"

"Well," said Pooh, "what I like best –" and then he had to stop and think. Because although Eating Honey *was* a very good thing to do, there was a moment just before you began to eat it which was better than when you were, but he didn't know what it was called. And then he thought that being with Christopher Robin was a very good thing to do, and having Piglet near was a very friendly thing to have; and so, when he had thought it all out, he said, "What I like best in the whole world is Me and Piglet going to see You, and You saying 'What about a little something?' and Me saying, 'Well, I shouldn't mind a little something, should you, Piglet,' and it being a hummy sort of day outside, and birds singing."

"I like that too," said Christopher Robin, "but what I like *doing* best is Nothing."

"How do you do Nothing?" asked Pooh, after he had wondered for a long time.

"Well, it's when people call out at you just as you're going off to do it, 'What are you going to do, Christopher Robin?' and you say 'Oh, nothing,' and then you go and do it."

"Oh, I see," said Pooh.

"This is a nothing sort of thing that we're doing now."

"Oh, I see," said Pooh again.

"It means just going along, listening to all the things you can't hear, and not bothering."

"Oh!" said Pooh.

They walked on, thinking of This and That, and by-and-by they came to an enchanted place on the very top of the
Forest called Galleons Lap, which is sixty-something trees

in a circle; and Christopher Robin knew that it was enchanted because nobody had ever been able to count whether it was sixty-three or sixty-four, not even when he tied a piece of string round each tree after he had counted it. Being enchanted, its floor was not like the floor of the Forest, gorse and bracken and heather, but close-set grass, quiet and smooth and green. It was the only place in the Forest where you could sit down carelessly, without getting up again almost at once and looking for somewhere else. Sitting there they could see the whole world spread out until it reached the sky, and whatever there was all the world over was with them in Galleons Lap.

Suddenly Christopher Robin began to tell Pooh about some of the things: People called Kings and Queens and something called Factors, and a place called Europe, and an island in the middle of the sea where no ships came, and how you make a Suction Pump (if you want to), and when Knights were Knighted, and what comes from Brazil. And 57

Pooh, his back against one of the sixty-something trees, and his paws folded in front of him, said "Oh!" and "I don't know," and thought how wonderful it would be to have a Real Brain which could tell you things. And by-and-by Christopher Robin came to an end of the things, and was silent, and he sat there looking out over the world, and wishing it wouldn't stop.

But Pooh was thinking too, and he said suddenly to Christopher Robin:

"Is it a very Grand thing to be an Afternoon, what you said?"

"A what?" said Christopher Robin lazily, as he listened to something else.

"On a horse?" explained Pooh.

"A Knight?"

"Oh, was that it?" said Pooh. "I thought it was a – Is it as Grand as a King and Factors and all the other things you said?"

"Well, it's not as grand as a King," said Christopher Robin, and then, as Pooh seemed disappointed, he added quickly, "but it's grander than Factors."

"Could a Bear be one?"

"Of course he could!" said Christopher Robin. "I'll make you one." And he took a stick and touched Pooh on the shoulder, and said, "Rise, Sir Pooh de Bear, most faithful of all my Knights."

So Pooh rose and sat down and said "Thank you," which is the proper thing to say when you have been made a Knight, and he went into a dream again, in which he and Sir Pump and Sir Brazil and Factors lived together with a horse, and were faithful knights (all except Factors, who looked after the horse) to Good King Christopher Robin ... and every now and then he shook his head, and said to himself, "I'm not getting it right." Then he began to think of all the things Christopher Robin would want to tell him when he came back from wherever he was going to, and how muddling it would be for a Bear of Very Little Brain to try and get them right in his mind. "So, perhaps," he said sadly to himself, "Christopher Robin won't tell me any more," and he wondered if being a Faithful Knight meant that you just went on being faithful without being told things.

Then, suddenly again, Christopher Robin, who was still looking at the world with his chin in his hands, called out "Pooh!"

"Yes?" said Pooh.
"When I'm – when – Pooh!"
"Yes, Christopher Robin?"
"I'm not going to do Nothing any more."
"Never again?"
"Well, not so much. They don't let you."

Pooh waited for him to go on, but he was silent again.

"Yes, Christopher Robin?" said Pooh helpfully.

"Pooh, when I'm – *you* know – when I'm *not* doing Nothing, will you come up here sometimes?"

"Just Me?"

"Yes, Pooh."

"Will you be here too?"

"Yes, Pooh, I will be really. I *promise* I will be, Pooh."

"That's good," said Pooh.

"Pooh, *promise* you won't forget about me, ever. Not even when I'm a hundred."

Pooh thought for a little.

"How old shall *I* be then?"

"Ninety-nine."

Pooh nodded.

"I promise," he said.

Still with his eyes on the world Christopher Robin put out a hand and felt for Pooh's paw.

"Pooh," said Christopher Robin earnestly, "if I – if I'm not quite –" he stopped and tried again – "Pooh, *whatever* happens, you *will* understand, won't you?"

"Understand what?"

"Oh, nothing." He laughed and jumped to his feet. "Come on!"

"Where?" said Pooh.

"Anywhere," said Christopher Robin.

So they went off together. But wherever they go, and whatever happens to them on the way, in that enchanted place on the top of the Forest a little boy and his Bear will always be playing.

The House at Pooh Corner

*If you have enjoyed this little
smackeral, you will also enjoy...*

Also available:

Hunnypot Library Colour Story Books (for small paws)

1855915448	*Piglet is Rescued* £1.99
1855915456	*A Party for Winnie-the-Pooh* £1.99
1855915464	*A House for Eeyore* £1.99
1855915472	*Tigger has Breakfast* £1.99
1855915650	*The Search for Small* £1.99
1855915669	*Tiggers Don't Climb Trees* £1.99
1855915677	*Rabbit's Busy Day* £1.99
1855915685	*Pooh Invents a New Game* £1.99

Padded Board Books (for very small paws)

0416193390	*Pooh Looks for Honey* £3.99
0416193404	*Piglet has an Adventure* £3.99
0416193412	*Eeyore has a Happy Day* £3.99
0416193420	*Tigger Bounces Home* £3.99

Cloth Books (for the smallest paws)

0416191517	*Pooh's Friends* £3.50
0416191525	*Pooh at Home* £3.50

AVAILABLE FROM ALL GOOD BOOK SHOPS
Prices shown above are the recommended retail prices
which were correct at the time of going to press.

WIN A POOH LIBRARY!

NOW WE ARE SEVENTY – Pooh's Prize Paw Draw
(UK and Eire residents only)

Winnie-the-Pooh will be seventy years old on October 14, 1996, and Reed Books are giving away 10 Pooh Libraries to help celebrate this Very Important Event. Each Pooh Library contains the colour classic hardback editions of *Winnie-the-Pooh*, *The House at Pooh Corner*, *When We Were Very Young* and *Now We Are Six* in a special gift box worth over £45. To enter the draw, simply fill out the coupon (a photocopy is acceptable) and post it to the address below to reach us by the closing date of January 31, 1997. The first 10 entries to be drawn from Eeyore's Useful Pot will each win a Pooh Library.

Now Post to: Pooh 70 Draw, Reed Books, Michelin House
81 Fulham Road, London, SW3 6RB

Small's Print 1) This competition draw is open to all residents of UK and Eire except for employees and associates of Reed Elsevier Plc, and their immediate families. 2) Only one entry per person. 3) The closing date is Jan 31, 1997. The draw will take place on Feb 3, 1997. Winners will be notified by post no later than Feb 28, 1997. 4) No cash alternative to the prizes allocated is available. Reed Books reserves the right to offer substitute prizes of similar value should the specified prizes become unavailable for reasons beyond our control. 5) Entrants' information will be used for market research purposes, but will *not* be passed on to outside organisations. 6) The Judges' decision is final. No correspondence will be entered into. 7) By entering the competition the entrants have agreed to be bound by the rules.

- -

Name .... **Age** ....

Address ....

....

.... **Postcode** ....

Where did you buy this book? ....